Righteous P.I.

Ross Thompson

Published by Ross Thompson, 2023.

RIGHTEOUS P.I.

First edition. September 7, 2023.

Copyright © 2023 Ross Thompson.

ISBN: 979-8223332053

Written by Ross Thompson.

Table of Contents

CHAPTER ONE

The signwriter had just left with my cheque in his pocket. He had done a great job. Charles Winston Private Investigations in elegant gold lettering with a hint of black background shadow, on the top panel of the office door. He was not head-over-heels with delight at having to accept my cheque.

"I would prefer cash if it's at all possible Mr. Winston."

"I do not have that much cash on me George. I keep the cash I carry to a bare minimum these days. How about online? Do you have a PayPal account?" The look on his face told me the answer was no. "Stripe? No. If you give me your Bank details, I will transfer the amount within the hour." Negative there also.

Officially, I am open for business on this first day of the new business. I put a small advertisement in a local weekly paper, but I was hoping for a grace period before anyone came knocking. I have scribbled down tasks to do on a notepad: 'Desk and leather chairs receive delivery of, small renovations, make the place presentable.' Got to fix this place up before I scare off any potential clients. I take a deep breath and wander to the window, looking down at the street below.

My office is on the second floor of a brick building in the heart of a middle-class neighbourhood. The building's old, made of red bricks that have seen better days. My window's dusty, but it frames a slice of everyday suburbia. The windows of the office are tall and wide, allowing ample natural light to filter in. Outside, the street is lined with neatly trimmed trees, their branches swaying gently in the breeze. Patches of well-manicured lawns stretch out between the sidewalks and the curbs.

The houses on either side of the street are diverse in design. A small, quaint park sits at the end of the block, offering a splash of greenery and a place for the local children to play. A wrought-iron fence surrounds the park. A green oasis where kids and dogs create their own kind of magic.

How did I get here? I Spent years in the force, chasing down every lowlife and crook in the city. Seen it all – the lies, the betrayals, the desperation. I was good at it, too. But the brass never liked my methods. Too unconventional, they said. And I was up to here with their bureaucracy, their politics. So, I cut ties, hung up my badge, and decided to do things my way. No red tape, no compromises. Just me, and my gut.

Moved on to work for the Private Investigation Companies. I had my fair share of sleuthing shenanigans working for those private investigation suits. But eventually, I decided it was time to hang up my magnifying glass and go solo.

First off, those company bigwigs had more layers than an onion. Every case I cracked, they were right there with their corporate machinations, trying to spin things into a tidy little PR package. Then there were the clients. Oh boy, the clients. Half of them thought they were in some kind of noir flick, with me as their Sam Spade. The other half treated me like I was their personal errand boy with a trench coat. I had enough of being everyone's go to boy. I wanted to pick the cases that got my blood pumping, not just the ones that tickled someone's fancy.

Ethics? Yeah, well, that's a can of worms. The company had its shady moments, and I'm not about to compromise my values for a paycheck. Going solo means I can do right by the clients without answering to some higher-ups who only care about the bottom line.

And don't even get me started on the hours. Running on their clock meant I had no life outside those four walls. Starting my own shop lets me run things on my terms – when I want to work and when I want to kick back.

The success I pull in now is not padding some company's pockets; it's lining mine.

So, I packed up my fedora and trench coat, and hung my own shingle. Now I'm the master of my destiny, the ruler of my own case files. Sure, it's a bit of a wild ride running my own show, but hey, at least I'm the one calling the shots. Running my own gig gives me the freedom to call the shots – pick the cases I want to sink my teeth into, do things my way. I needed to work for folks who appreciated the skills I bring to the table, not treat me like some hired help. So, there you have it – no more corporate strings, no more client nonsense, just me, my skills, and the road ahead.

On top of all that the office coffee was always bad. So, I decided if I had to drink mediocre coffee, it would be of my own production

CHAPTER TWO

Amidst all the grit and toughness, there is one part of me that folks wouldn't expect – my faith. It's not something I talk about much, but it is there, a flicker of something deeper, I became a Christian almost against my will. Back in the days when I thought I was bulletproof, life threw me a curveball.

I was facing a case that had me questioning everything. There was this darkness that I could not shake, a weight that felt too heavy to bear alone. I found myself in the quiet corners of a church, seeking something I did not fully understand. It wasn't like I suddenly had a lightbulb moment or a divine revelation. No, it was more like a slow realization that I needed more than just my own strength.

I remember the nights spent wrestling with my demons, the anger, and the frustration. Yeah, it was a battle. I fought against it. Fought against the idea of needing something greater. But bit by bit, the walls I had built around myself started to crumble. It wasn't weakness that brought me to my knees – it was the realization that even the toughest of us need something to hold onto, especially when the world gets dark. As I look back, I can see how that reluctant acceptance changed me.

I did not become soft or preachy. My faith didn't erase the edge that's kept me alive on the streets. If anything, it sharpened my focus, gave me an anchor in the chaos. So, amidst the toughness, amidst the grind, there is this ember of belief that keeps burning. A belief that there is a higher power, even in the grime and the shadows.

I shake my head, chuckling softly at the irony of it all. Who would've thought? Me, a hard-nosed detective, finding something to believe in beyond the cases and the scum. But hey, life's full of surprises, isn't it?

And yeah, I've been called a lot of things in my time, but I like to think of myself these days as the righteous P.I. Not because I am any better than the next guy or because I'm walking around with some holier-than-thou attitude. No, it's because the Good Book says that if anybody receives Jesus, well, God calls them righteous – like it or not. So, while I'm navigating the shadows of this city, I am just striving to honour that title the best way I know how.

CHAPTER THREE

Of course, as I stand here looking at this place, I realize I have inadvertently done the very thing that is likely to draw in customers. I could sit around all day waiting for the phone to ring or watching the door, and no one would show up. But the moment you have something to do, something you do not want interrupted, it's a sure-fire guarantee that somebody will turn up, knocking on your door, wanting something from you. It's like a law of nature or something.

The jingle of the bell above the door proved me right and announced the arrival of a new figure. Stepping into my office, the light caught the edges of a fedora that cast a shadow over his face. I lifted my gaze and observed the newcomer.

His eyes, a deep shade of blue, hold a mixture of weariness and determination. Our gazes locked.

He was a middle-aged businessman with a slightly hunched posture, his shoulders tense and slightly slumped as if carrying the weight of his concerns. His once neatly pressed suit is now slightly wrinkled, the tie loosened and askew. His salt-and-pepper hair meticulously combed, yet there is an unruly strand that stubbornly refuses to stay in place. Deep lines etch his forehead, evidence of countless hours spent furrowing his brows in thought.

His eyes, carry a hint of fatigue and worry. They dart around the room, occasionally locking onto something before quickly shifting elsewhere. Dark circles have formed beneath his eyes, testament to many sleepless nights spent wrestling with his concerns. He absentmindedly taps his fingers against his thigh, a nervous habit that betrays his inner turmoil.

As he talks, his voice carries a touch of anxiety, the words coming out a bit faster than usual, occasionally stumbling over themselves. He gestures with his hands, but the movements lack their usual confidence and precision. His lips purse together in a thoughtful expression, and he lets out a heavy sigh every now and then, as if trying to release the weight of his worries through his breath.

Despite his efforts to maintain composure, there is an underlying sense of vulnerability that peeks through. It is as if he is struggling to find solutions to the challenges he is facing. His overall appearance speaks of a man who is grappling with the pressures of life, unsure of how things will unfold and deeply concerned about the outcomes.

He comes straight to the point, "I've heard you're the best in town," the man began, his words deliberate. "Name's Samuel Blackwood. I need someone who knows how to handle himself out there on the street."

My lips formed a slight smirk. "I think I'm your man, Mr. Blackwood."

Leaning forward, he narrowed his eyes, gauging my reaction. "I need you to find my sister," he said flatly. "She disappeared a week ago without a trace. The police don't seem to care, but I know something's off."

My interest was piqued. Missing persons cases were never straightforward; they held hidden layers waiting to be unravelled. I nodded. I pulled up two chairs into the centre of the empty room motioning for him to take a seat in the chair across from me.

"I was not expecting to start business for a few days yet. I can't offer you much in the way of comfort at present. I can give you a coffee if you would like one."

Samuel Blackwood shook his head. "My sister Amalie is a journalist. She is not your average woman. She was onto something big – a pharmaceutical corporation's illegal activities. She had evidence, information that could expose them. She was digging deep, getting closer to the truth."

My eyebrows raised. The combination of corporate intrigue and a missing person suggested a puzzle of complexities. "And you believe her disappearance is connected to her investigation?"

Blackwood's jaw tightened briefly, a hint of anger flashing across his features. "Yes, I do. She became paranoid, cautious about discussing her findings over the phone. She thought she was being followed. And then two days ago, she vanished."

His gaze never wavered. "I think the deeper she went, the more dangerous it got. I need you to find out what happened to her."

I nodded, mentally connecting the dots. This was more than a missing person case, a conspiracy intertwined with the corporate world. A path fraught with peril that could lead me into deep water.

"Rest assured, Mr. Blackwood, I'll do everything in my power to locate your sister and uncover the truth behind her disappearance. I will need email and phone contact details from you. Give me twenty-four hours and I'll contact you for more information."

He agreed to my fee structure which included expenses, signed an agreement. We shook hands and he left. I had my first case.

CHAPTER FOUR

I figured the ladies boss, her editor, was the first person to see. I met him at the offices of the Daily Inquirer.

"Thanks for seeing me Mr Bell. I'm a private detective." I handed him my new business card. "I've been asked by Amalie Blackwood's family to look into her disappearance."

He seemed relieved someone was doing something. "It's a troubling situation. Amalie is an excellent journalist, but she often chased after dangerous stories. I was always warning her about the risks."

"Can you fill me in on the story she was working on before she disappeared?"

"It concerned a pharmaceutical Company, Medico-Pharma. She believed they were involved in some shady practices, including covering up the side effects of their latest drug. She thought it had caused harm to some patients."

"And did she share any details with you about her findings or her plans for the investigation?""

"She did share some initial findings with me. I saw some documents that raised serious questions about the validity of their clinical trials, potential off-label marketing, and even possible bribery of medical professionals. But I warned her, Detective. I told her that this was dangerous territory, and she should be cautious. Amalie was quite secretive about her work, even with me. She mentioned a few leads, some insider sources she was talking to, but she never disclosed all the information she had. She believed that if she kept things close to her chest, she would be safer."

"Did you advise her against pursuing this story?"

"Absolutely, I did. I warned her that investigating powerful corporations like Medico-Pharma could be dangerous. These companies have resources to protect their interests. I said she should consider her safety first."

"What was her response to your warning?"

"Amalie was dedicated and passionate about her work. She told me she could not just let this slide – that it was her duty as a journalist to uncover the truth, no matter how uncomfortable it might be. I knew she was treading on thin ice. But she was adamant that the public needed to know about this, and I respected her determination.

Amalie has that unwavering determination that most successful investigative journalists possess. She believed in exposing the truth, no matter the cost. I respected her commitment, but she was wading out into hazardous waters."

"Did she receive any threats or face any unusual incidents before she disappeared?"

"He nodded." She did mention a few instances of receiving anonymous emails warning her to back off. There was also an odd car following her a couple of times. But you know how journalists can be – Amalie brushed it off as part of the territory. She was stubbornly focused on her mission."

"Did she have any personal involvement with Medico-Pharma, outside her pursuit of the story?"

He shook his head. "Not as far as I know."

"Ok Mr Bell, thank you for seeing me. I'll be in touch if I need further assistance."

He shook my hand. "Anytime."

As I left the building, I mused on the editors' words. He had used words like passionate, dedicated. Said Amalie believed the public had a right to know. She was the lone crusader whose job it was to expose these felons. Personally, I call it naïve. Like the newspaper people who go to the war zones. Some don't come back. Some newspaper people have a cockeyed idea of the importance of their work. To me they are the same as the amateurs who go into remote areas and get lost or climb mountains and get into trouble. Experienced professionals then must risk their lives to rescue them.

Sure, if you discover foul play pass it on to the agencies equipped to handle those things. The Police. FBI, and the various Security Organisations. But to decide to be a lone vigilante, as Amalie was doing, when the total of your experience is the ability to write well, is plain dumb. The World has enough trouble in it, without putting yourself into circumstances that beckon it to you.

Amalie had bitten off more than she could chew, and people like me get dragged into the mix to find her. If she was still alive.

CHAPTER FIVE

Blackwood had given me permission to give Amalie's apartment the once over. I did not bother asking for a key. It was not difficult, with a bit of dexterity, to get in.

I stepped into Amelia Blackwood's flat, I moved cautiously through the living room. That I was not the first visitor was obvious. A professional I guessed since the door gave no sign of forced entry. Signs of disturbance were everywhere. Books piled haphazardly on the coffee table, a chair pushed askew, and a stack of papers lay scattered across the floor. Someone had been here, and they had not been careful about concealing it.

I knelt to examine the papers. Among them were notes, articles, and printouts – a chaotic collection of Amelia's journalistic work. One thing was glaringly obvious – no sign of a computer of any sort.

As I continued to scan the room, my eyes fell upon the bookshelf. A gap stood out like a missing tooth, a void where something had been removed.

A quick search of the rest of the apartment yielded more evidence of intrusion. In her study, the filing cabinet was ajar, folders half-pulled out and left in disarray. The desk drawers emptied of their contents, and the floor littered with bits of paper and scattered pens. It was as if someone had been frantically searching for something, tearing the place apart in the process.

I pulled on a pair of gloves and crouched beside the desk, sifting through the mess. There, beneath a pile of papers, I found a small, discreet bug – a listening device planted to eavesdrop on Amelia's conversations. Someone had been keeping tabs on her, waiting for the right opportunity to strike.

No doubt about it, Amelie's investigations into the pharmaceutical Companies malpractice had struck a nerve. They had been here, tearing apart her life, taking her laptop and documents, likely to erase any evidence of her work and the identities of her sources.

The apartments condition said these people were dangerous, and they were desperate.

I was about to enter the bedroom. I was standing near a window. a glint of light caught my eye. Through the half-opened blinds, I spotted a sleek, black sedan parked across the street. Two figures sat inside, their posture casual, but the intent behind their presence was anything but innocent. I had attracted somebody's attention.

Being the kind of guy who doesn't back down easily, I figured it was time to confront the folks in that parked car. I mean, they were watching me like hawks, and I was not about to let them think I was an easy mark. I headed straight for the door.

As I stepped out onto the sidewalk, my eyes locked onto that sleek black sedan. The sun was casting long shadows, giving everything an extra layer of tension. I could see the two figures inside, acting all cool, but I could practically smell trouble wafting off them. Nobody does surveillance on me without answering some questions.

With a determined stride, I crossed the street and headed straight for the car. As I got closer, I made sure to meet their gaze, letting them know I was ticked off. I could see a flicker of surprise in their eyes – they probably didn't expect me to come right at them.

I leaned against the car, letting a sly grin creep onto my face. "You guys lost or something?" I quipped, my voice dripping with that mixture of confidence and curiosity. The occupants exchanged a quick glance before the one in the driver's seat rolled the window down a little more.

"We're just taking in the sights," the driver replied, his tone casual but guarded.

I raised an eyebrow, not buying it for a second. "Sights, huh? Must be some pretty thrilling sights in this part of town" My words hung in the air, a subtle challenge to reveal their true intentions.

The guy in the passenger seat shifted uncomfortably, his eyes narrowing slightly. "Look, we're not causing any trouble. Just minding our own business."

I chuckled, not bothering to hide my scepticism. "Minding your own business by tailing me? That's a new approach."

The tension in the car was palpable now, and I could practically taste their unease. I leaned in a little closer, my voice lowering to a gravelly whisper. "Here's the deal. I don't take kindly to being watched. So, how about you spill the beans on who you're working for and what you want, before things get ugly?"

The window went up abruptly, the engine fired up, and the vehicle rolled away. I straightened up, a satisfied grin playing on my lips. It looked like my little game of chicken had worked, as I watched them pull away from the curb.

I went back inside and resumed my perusal of Amalie's apartment. The door to Amelia's bedroom was open. I could see drawers pulled out; clothes tossed aside – it was a scene of thorough upheaval. A window was open. A gust of wind ruffled the curtain

The moment I stepped into that dimly lit bedroom I felt something taut against my shin. A hair-thin wire stretched across the doorway at ankle height. Somebody's intending to turn this place into a death-trap. Then it struck me, those boys outside were waiting to confirm an explosion to their bosses.

I am no stranger to danger, but this is a whole new level of lowdown trickery. This wire is not just there to annoy, it is there to make me trip headfirst into whatever they have cooked up on the other side.

I swallow hard, my throat dry as the Sahara. I take a step back, careful not to disturb that wire. As I carefully examine the fine wire stretched across the bedroom doorway, my eyes trace its path to the source. It leads to a small, inconspicuous device nestled against the wall near the door frame. The device is a contraption of wires, switches, and a timer of some sort.

I crouch down, examining that wire. My heart raced, adrenaline pumping through my veins, as I assessed the explosive charge connected to the trip wire. The first task was to identify the type of explosive. Careful examination revealed a compact device, wires meticulously intertwined, connected to a small container. My trained eyes recognized it as a potent concoction, one that could obliterate everything within a considerable radius. But I was not here to witness destruction; the task was to dismantle it.

I took a deep breath, my gloved hands steady and focused. Every move I made needed to be precise; a single misstep would set off a chain reaction that would leave nothing but destruction in its wake.

As I inch my way around the contraption, I notice a small panel on the side – a potential access point. With steady hands, I carefully open it, revealing a series of wires, circuits, and a blinking LED light. My gut tells me that disarming this will not be as simple as cutting a single wire.

I walked into the kitchen and found a large pair of scissors. It was a delicate operation; I had to sever the connection without disturbing the balance. One wrong move, and the lights would go out.

Gently, I positioned the scissors and with a steady hand, snipped the wire. The faintest sound of metal against metal resonated in the room. A bead of sweat trickled down my forehead, and I wiped it away before it could betray my nerves.

With the connection severed, my attention turned back to the explosive device. My fingers worked nimbly, extracting wires with a surgeon's precision. Each wire removed was a step closer to safety, and my focus intensified with every successful disconnection. Time seemed to stand still, the only sound being the soft clicks of wires being detached.

Finally, the last wire dangled before me, and a wave of relief washed over me. But this was not over yet. My fingers danced over the intricate web of circuitry, disarming each component with deliberate care. As the final piece fell into my hand, I held my breath. The device was rendered harmless.

I stepped back from the dismantled explosive charge. The room seemed to breathe a sigh of relief alongside me. The danger was past, the trap neutralized, even as I felt a shiver down my spine at the thought of what could have been.

I put a call into the Police explaining the situation, whose apartment it was, that I had disarmed the device, and leaving my details. That would create some urgency in whatever they were doing to find Amalie Blackwood and add to the pressure on her kidnappers.

CHAPTER SIX

Sam Blackwood, on my return call, had told me a fellow reporter, David Miller, was Amalie's closest friend. I arranged to meet him at a coffee place near his work.

According to David, their conversation had taken place one evening. Amelia had reached out to him, her voice tinged with concern. She confided in him about the sensitive information she had dug up on the pharmaceutical company's alleged illegal activities. She feared that her investigation had placed her in harm's way.

As David recounted it to me, he had advised her to be cautious, to take steps to ensure her safety. He even offered to meet up in person, in order to brainstorm potential safety measures they could put in place. However, Amelia saw no need for that. She assured David that she had taken precautions and was being careful.

I asked David about their conversation in more detail during our interview.

"So, David," I began, leaning forward slightly, "what did she say exactly? About the information and her concerns?"

David looked pensive; his brows furrowed as he recalled the conversation. "Well, we talked for a while. She was worried, you know, about what she had uncovered. She told me she had solid evidence of the pharmaceutical company's wrongdoing. She felt like she was onto something big, something dangerous."

I nodded, urging him to continue.

"And what did you advise her?"

David let out a sigh, running a hand through his hair. "I told her to be careful, to not take any unnecessary risks. I suggested meeting up so we could figure out how to ensure her safety. But she was so stubborn, insisting that she had it all under control. Said she had taken steps to protect herself." His frustration was palpable, and I could tell he regretted not being able to persuade her otherwise.

"And when you realized she was missing, what did you do?"

David's eyes clouded with worry. "I tried calling her again and again. When she did not respond, I knew something was wrong. I contacted the authorities, told them about her investigation and our last conversation. I knew something had happened."

During the conversation David Miller mentioned Amalie had a jogging routine twice weekly at a local park. I asked if he had time to show me the track and walk some of it with me. He agreed and we did the short trip in my car.

The morning sun cast a faint golden hue over the park as we walked side by side along the winding jogging track. The idea was to scan both sides of the track for anything unusual. " "Keep your eyes peeled David. We are looking for anything out of the ordinary.

We proceeded slowly for five minutes. As we passed through a stand of trees on both sides of the path, I saw it. "Wait," I commanded softly, both of us stopped abruptly. I pointed to a piece of jewellery, a broach, half-hidden in the grass, silver and sparkling despite its inconspicuous placement.

Miller's breath hitched audibly, his eyes widening as he recognized the necklace. His voice held a mixture of relief and anguish as he confirmed, "That's hers. It's definitely hers."

I crouched down and carefully pick it up. I stood up. As I examined it, I said, "Every detail matters. We'll analyse this and see where it leads us. It looks as though they grabbed her here. The trees provide enough cover for it to be done quickly."

Miller's hands clenched into fists, his emotions evident in the lines of his face. He looked around the park with a mix of desperation and determination, as if expecting answers to materialize from thin air.

Miller met my gaze, his determination mirrored in his eyes. "Thank you for doing this," he said, his voice filled with gratitude and a hint of desperation.

I gave him a nod. "Let's keep moving."

I drove David back to the Inquirer building. "You've been a big help, David. If there is anything else, you remember don't hesitate to call me."

He nodded his gaze distant. "I just hope she's okay, you know?"

I suppose I should have been more honest with David. I would not be getting the broach analysed. There was no point. It had obviously come off in the struggle. It would have no fingerprints other than Amalie's, from her daily handling of the thing.

CHAPTER SEVEN

As I drove back to the office following my appointment with David, it began to rain. I looked in my rear-view mirror. The black sedan. They were at it again. My knuckles tightened around the leather-wrapped steering wheel as I took a hard left onto the rain-slicked streets, the roar of the engine reverberating through the narrow alleyways. The city lights blurred into streaks of neon as I pushed the accelerator to the floor, the gritty pavement a canvas for the adrenaline-fueled dance that was about to unfold.

I stole a quick glance in the rear-view mirror, catching a glimpse of the dark sedan tailing me with a persistence that only emboldened my resolve. They thought they could keep up; thought they could rattle me. But they didn't know who they were dealing with. I had been around this block before.

The rhythmic thumping of the rain against the windshield matched the pounding of my heart, each drop a staccato beat urging me forward. The city was a maze, and I was the rat racing through it.

With a flick of the wheel, I veered onto a wider avenue, the headlights of the pursuing car dancing in my peripheral vision. I could practically feel their desperation, their determination to close the gap. But I had a few tricks up my sleeve, and it was time to play my hand.

As I approached a T-junction, I slammed on the brakes, my car skidding sideways as I executed a hair-raising 180-degree spin. The pursuing sedan swerved, tires screeching in protest, as they struggled to match my manoeuvre, but I was already back on the gas, hurtling down a new street before they could regain their bearings.

The urban canyon of buildings and billboards flashed past me, a chaotic symphony of lights and shadows. I knew this city like the back of my hand – every alley, every shortcut, every hidden nook. And I was putting that knowledge to good use. I took a sharp right into a narrow alley, the walls closing in around me. My heart raced as I pushed my car to the limit, the pursuing sedan hot on my tail. But I had one last trick to pull, one last roll of the dice.

With a guttural roar, I accelerated toward a makeshift ramp at the end of the alley, my car's tires leaving the ground as I sailed through the air. Time seemed to slow as I cleared the gap, the world a surreal blur of motion and lights. The impact on the other side was bone-jarring, but I gritted my teeth and fought to regain control.

I landed with a thud and screeched around a corner, my tires smoking as I fishtailed onto a main road. Behind me, the pursuing car was not so lucky – they had underestimated the gap and crashed into a stack of crates, their chase coming to an abrupt and spectacular end.

I glanced in the rear-view mirror, a triumphant grin spreading across my face. The city lights glinted off my wet windshield, and for a moment, I felt like I was on top of the world. They were just another set of wheels fading into the distance.

I eased off the accelerator, the adrenaline slowly giving way to a sense of satisfaction. As I navigated the city's labyrinthine streets, I had made my point. And as the rain continued to fall, washing away the evidence of the chase, I could not help but relish the sweet taste of victory.

CHAPTER EIGHT

The office phone was ringing as I stepped out of the lift. So much for a few days breathing space. I hurried in and picked it up. "Hello, Charles Winston Investigations."

The voice was low and menacing. Well, well, well, what do we have here? The nosy detective poking around where he shouldn't be.""

"Who is this?

"Names aren't important right now. What's important is that you back off. You're messing with things that are way above your pay grade."

"I'm just trying to find out what happened to that journalist."

You have no idea what you are getting into. Let me make it clear for you: drop this case or there will be consequences. You don't want to see what happens when people don't listen to reason."

"Threats are par for the course in the work I do. When I uncover the truth, I'll back off."

"Truth? Truth can be a slippery thing, detective. You think you're some kind of hero, but you're just a bug crawling around, and I can squash you anytime I want."

"Threats won't deter me. You are wasting your breath."

A chuckle. "You've got guts, I'll give you that. But let me paint you a picture. You keep digging, and you won't just be putting your life on the line. I've got connections, detective. Connections that reach places you can't even imagine."

"I have a few connections myself. Connections on the right side of the law. If you had any hand in that journalist's disappearance, I will expose you too."

The voice turned cold. "You're treading on thin ice, detective. You don't know who you are up against. You won't see me coming, but you'll feel the consequences if you keep going."

"Attempts at intimidation are just another day at the office in the work I do."

Now he was angry. "You've sealed your fate, detective. You had a choice, but you've made it. Remember, you were warned."

"I'll take my chances. Give it your best shot."

The phone went dead.

I put the phone down. The cockroaches were coming into the daylight.

CHAPTER NINE

My inbox had an email from a Janice O'Malley. 'Hi Mr Winston. I am a friend of Amalie Blackwood. Sam Blackwood told me he had hired you to find Amalie. Amalie left a post bag with me three weeks ago. I prefer not to be seen with you. If you agree I will leave the envelope in the lower branches of an oak tree at Camden crossroads tomorrow morning.'

Camden is a small village twenty kilometres into the country beyond the city outskirts. Camden crossroads, two kilometres this side of the village. I replied with 'Ok, I will be there around 11am.'

The scene at the crossroads is one of rustic charm and natural beauty, transporting anyone who happens upon it into a simpler and more tranquil world. The air carries a faint scent of wildflowers and earth, creating a soothing atmosphere that invites a moment of respite. Tall, swaying grasses line the edges of the roads. Standing sentinel are ancient oak trees, their gnarled branches reaching skyward, their leaves rustle softly in the wind. A simple wooden signpost stands at the centre of the crossroads, pointing travellers in the direction of nearby villages, farms, and places of interest.

The post bag held a strong box key with a tag of the Fidelity Savings and Trust Bank in the city.

I did not have to give any ID at the Bank. A note with the box stipulated any person producing the key could open it. I lifted the lid and found a notebook inside. Its pages filled with meticulous notes, detailing the reporter's investigation into the company's shady dealings. Flipping through the pages revealed why my probing had stirred the beehive.

Amalie had listed a formidable array of offences by Medico-Pharma. Off-Label Marketing, Clinical Trials Manipulation, Bribery and Kickbacks, Price Fixing, Data Breaches, Unlawful Influence on Regulators, and Failure to Disclose Side Effects, and illegal sales.

All of which revealed a pursuit of the dollar by illegal means with not the slightest concern for the end user, the consumer. Such people are driven by unbridled greed and self-interest. This character places financial gain above all else, callously exploiting the vulnerabilities of others for personal enrichment.

This is not your run-of-the-mill hustler or two-bit con artist. No, this guy's a different breed altogether. He's the kind who would sell his own soul for a fat wallet and wouldn't even blink. His addiction is cold, hard cash. The green stuff talks, and it is singing a siren song that only he can hear. This city's full of marks, suckers, and losers just begging to be parted from their earnings, and he is more than happy to oblige.

He preys on the weak, the desperate, and the naive. Sick kids? Elderly widows? Small businesses struggling to stay afloat? They are all just potential revenue streams to him. His moral compass? That thing is rusted to oblivion. He cannot even tell the difference between right and wrong anymore.

I have tangled with all sorts of lowlifes in my time, these guys are in a league of their own. Venomous snakes, predators who wear a three-piece suit instead of fangs.

This guy's got a moral compass that is so skewed, it's like he's operating in a different dimension. He sees vulnerabilities in folks the way a vulture spots roadkill on a hot summer day. He preys on desperation, exploits the broken dreams and shattered hopes of those who cross his path, all for one thing: his pocketbook.

You would think he'd have a lick of remorse, a smidgen of guilt somewhere deep down in that blackened heart of his, but nope, it is like he's been carved from stone, stone cold to the core. He will step on anyone, anywhere, anytime, as long as the dollar notes keep rolling in.

He does not know it but he is pitting himself against God... It may take a while but eventually the only thing he'll be counting' is the bars on his cell

Closing the notebook with care, I secured it in my bag. On the way out I handed back the key and informed the clerk the box would no longer be needed. I was still going around in circles. The notebook was not a great deal of use to me in my main interest: finding Amalie Blackwood. I would forward it to the Police with another explanatory note and my details.

CHAPTER TEN

It was time to go to Jo Jo's. Jo Jo's is where I go to think. Experience has taught me in this business, thinking is as important as action. Time spent in kicking back and allowing the mind to mull over the various aspects of a case, is far more important than running around like a headless chook.

Jo Jo's is a coffee and light meals establishment about a kilometre from the office. I have always gone there twice a week when I am working. They know me as a regular. I have deliberately kept my contact there to a superficial level. "How are you? Having the same?" "Yes thanks, how is business?" "Could be better." They do not know my name or what I do. I walked the kilometre, intending to spend an hour at Jo Jo's drinking coffee and eating something small, then walking home. All the while letting the case percolate in my grey matter. It did not quite work out that way.

Leaving a note on the door - back in one hour – I pocketed my door key, rode the elevator down, and walked out to the street. At Jo Jo's a waiter I had not seen before materialised, a lanky fellow with slicked back black hair and a welcoming grin.

"Cappuccino with one sugar please." I handed him a small note and he was gone, returning five minutes later with the coffee and the change. I signalled for him to keep the change.

"Thanks."

The place was close to full. I became aware I had to use the toilet. I'm older now. The plumbing is working fine, but these days when I need to go, I need to go. I knew where the toilets were, down an entrance way to the left of the main counter.

I worked my way through the tables acknowledging the occasional smile directed at me. The toilets were always spotlessly clean. After doing my business I threaded my way back to my coffee. It would be cooling by now. I lifted the cup and finished it, intending to order another. That is where my memory stops.

I came back to consciousness, lying on my back in pitch blackness, dense and alarming. My breathing in short fast breaths. My mind raced, searching for answers, attempting to make sense of the situation. Where was I? What had happened? I recalled the café, my returning from the restroom, finishing the almost cold coffee, then nothing. I sat up, then clambered to my feet. I had been lying on straw, a lot of straw. I moved slowly forward arms outstretched. Eventually I contacted the formidable massive roughness of stonework, cold and immovable. I moved around the wall hand over hand until I had established, I was in a small room or cell, about two meters on each side. The entire floor covered in a thick layer of straw.

Then, along with a heavy feeling in my stomach, it came to me. Knock out drops of some sort had been dropped in the coffee while I was away. By following the wall, I found the door. A heavy steel door with no opening mechanisms on my side.

I struggled to come to terms with this brutal new reality. I had been relaxed, blissful, enjoying a cup of coffee, and now disoriented, panicked, in a pitch-black stone cell. I continued in this agitated state for some time, struggling to bring some stability into my mind, body, and soul.

Without warning a small amount of light came under the door. Someone was coming. The light grew brighter, and I heard the person doing what was necessary on the outside to open the door. The door creaked loudly as it swung open. A figure walked in with a torch. I could see nothing of him except that he was about my height and wearing a bandana on his head.

He swung the torch around until he located me, then he walked towards me. I could not see if he had a weapon of any sort. It was an unconscious response on my part. A moment of instant decision. A survival response. As he drew close, I grabbed the torch out of his hand and shone it directly into his eyes. I put all my strength into a roundhouse punch to his solar plexus. He dropped to his knees gasping for breath. I pushed him over sideways and gagged him with the bandana, tying it as tightly as I could at the back of his head. I stripped him of his wide leather belt, pulled his hands behind him, and did my best to tie an elaborate knot using the full length of the belt.

Beyond the cell door a narrow passageway snaked off into the distance. The walls the same stone as the cell. I saw light further up the corridor. I could hear voices. It was a room. The voices increased in volume as the men in the room walked out into the passageway.

I had nowhere to go! It occurred to me to look up at the ceiling. A wooden framework supported it. If I could get up there, I could rest on the beams. I started up the stone wall. It wasn't easy but provided just enough toe and hand holds to make progress. Near the top I lunged for the wood and managed get a firm grip, eventually hauling myself up onto the beams.

Torches came on as three men came down the passageway. I had closed and barred the cell door. They would think that strange since their friend had come down to open the door and presumably bring me out. Seeing the barred door all three came to a sudden halt like soldiers on a parade ground. Then rushing forward, they lifted the bar from the door, opened it and cautiously entered the cell. They found their friend quickly. I could hear them talking loudly in another language which could have been Italian.

Dropping to the floor I rushed forward and banged the bar down on the door. I took off through the labyrinth of passages looking for signs of light. I had to back track a few times but eventually saw the glimmer I was seeking. It came from the other side of a large wooden door. Thankfully, it opened onto the street. I stepped out into the sunshine.

They had not got around to taking anything from me. My office key was still in my pocket and so was my wallet. Customarily I had not taken my gun to Jo Jo's. I recognized the part of town I was in. I hopped a bus and rode for twenty minutes, before disembarking and going in search of a coffee place. For two reasons. I needed two strong cups, and it would help me climb back on the horse again. It would not do to develop a phobia about coffee places.

A lesson I knew but had let slip, had been reinforced the hard way. In my profession do not keep to routines even in the smallest things. If they know where you are going and when you will be there, you have handed them the advantage. No more Jo Jo's, not regularly anyway. I doubt whether the staff there had had a hand in the affair. Probably thought I had suddenly taken ill. Whoever carted me off would have had a good story. Racing me off to a doctor, or a hospital for example.

I reminded myself not to give up on the prayer for protection I prayed every morning. It kept coming to my mind the weirdness of my situation. I volunteered for this job – I wanted it. Why was I not working as an accountant, a taxi driver, or some other benign employment? Maybe I had a screw loose somewhere and did not recognize it. I filed that away for serious consideration at some future date.

CHAPTER ELEVEN

The delivery of my office furniture had occurred while I was incognito. The freight people had left it stacked up at the door. Two large leather office chairs and a heavy polished oak desk. I know it was heavy because it took me the best part of an hour of solo effort to manoeuvre it through the outer door, then the door to my office.

I never take my phone to Jo Jo's. The plan was thinking with no interruptions. An alert for a received text message was on the screen when I picked it up. From Reggie Beale, fellow private investigator. Reggie's reputation was not pristine. Whoever offered the greatest amount of money was Reggie's work regimen. Which side of the law they were on was not something Reggie gave much consideration too.

His text: 'Charles, I might have a lead for you, regarding Amalie Blackwood's disappearance.' We were to meet at an abandoned warehouse in a run-down part of town.

Yeah, sure Reggie! Still, it might give me a look at who I am up against. It was a dead cert Reggie would not be there alone. How could I make it blow up in Reggie's face and whoever was with him? I replied to Reggie in the affirmative.

I was to meet Reggie at 11am. I arrived at 9.30 am. At the third-floor level of a building across the street from the warehouse, I took up a position on a fixed fire escape. Although the building was not directly opposite the warehouse, I had an unhindered view of the entire place. At 10.00 am a Mercedes limousine pulled up at the rear of the warehouse. Reggie and four men in dark suits emerged.

It would be a safer bet than Pharlap to win, those four thugs had some exotic fire power in shoulder holsters under their jackets. Reggie was noticeably nervous. Perhaps he had been forced to contact me. Knowing they intended to finish me off probably added to his woes. Reggie was crooked but I doubt he would willingly participate in the sinister violence those four gorilla's intended. The limousine drove off. After a brief conversation the four hoods dispersed to positions in the dilapidated building and Reggie walked through to the front of the building.

At 10.45 am I descended the fire escape and walked to the pay phone fifty yards along the street. I placed a call to the Police emergency number. With my handkerchief over the handpiece and raising the pitch of my voice I did my best impression of an agitated woman reporting four armed men at the old warehouse who seemed to be holding another man prisoner. I waited two minutes before ringing again to make the same report in my own voice. I expressed the reluctance to identify myself common to most calls to the Police emergency number.

Then it was back to my perch on the fire escape to watch the show. I did not have to wait long. The tranquil facade of the Street was shattered by the blaring wail of sirens. Four police cars, each adorned with flashing red and blue lights, converged on the scene in a symphony of chaos. The emergency call had been vague, but the officers knew better than to underestimate the unpredictable nature of such situations. The lead car skidded to a stop in front of the warehouse. Simultaneously, the three patrol cars following, their tires screeching as they halted at awkward angles, creating an impromptu barricade. Doors swung open, officers spilling out like a controlled flood, each brandishing a weapon. An officer, obviously in charge, emerged from the first car barking orders.

As the officers assessed the situation, chaos reigned. A cacophony of shouting and shuffling filled the air, blending with the relentless sirens that seemed to reverberate through the very marrow of the street. The suburban calm had shattered, replaced by an electric energy that charged the atmosphere. Shouts mixed with the crackling of radios and the thud of boots against pavement. The leaders voice rang out, directing officers to "Hold your positions!" and "Contain the suspect!"

The suspect at that time was Reggie, standing transfixed, hands raised, mouth hanging open in surprize. A brief stand-off followed before the four goons appeared hands raised above their heads. A large black van rumbled up into which the four goons and Reggie were herded. It was a great show. I could not have asked for more. I know bogus calls to Police Emergency is frowned upon. My rationale was if the Police were not aware of these goons they should be. At the very least my call would acquaint the law with the malevolent four. If the decision were made to photograph and fingerprint them that would be a bonus. Reggie, of course, had plenty of mileage with the boys in blue. Unfortunately, apprehended in the company of such heavy-duty malcontents was certain to add a black mark on his file.

CHAPTER TWELVE

I was still chuckling to myself as I unlocked my office door. The smile dropped off my face when I looked behind the door. As a security measure I leave two empty boxes on the floor behind the door, close enough that opening it will nudge them without drawing the attention of an intruder. The boxes sit on a short line drawn on the floor with a black marker. Opening the door will nudge the books over the line. I open the door only enough for me to slip in without disturbing them. The boxes were well over the black line. Somebody had been here.

Now my senses are on high alert. After the trip wire in Amalie's apartment and the knockout drops, I am beginning to understand the full extent of the dangerous game I am caught up in.

Glancing around the room I can see nothing out of the ordinary, until I noticed a faint acrid scent lingering in the air. I could make no sense of that for fifteen minutes. Then my eyes settled on the doorknob of the door into the room where my desk was. A close inspection revealed a thin line of clear liquid had been carefully applied to it. A cold shiver ran down my spine, the hairs on my neck stood on end, as I recognized the sinister intent displayed there.

I had read on the internet of a poison applied to the front door of Russian absconders living in England. It did not kill them, but it came mighty close to doing so. I could be facing the same thing here. I moved cautiously around the place eventually satisfying myself of no other dangers.

I had a Scientist friend, Margaret Hansen, who had graciously looked into a few small things for me in the past. There was no way I was going to play around with that substance on the doorknob myself. Before contacting her though I swept the place for bugs. Whoever had entered here was sure to have deposited a bug or two. I did not want them listening to my conversation with Margaret for a start. My bug sweeper located one under my desk and a second high on the window in the reception area.

With a sigh, I pulled out my phone and dialled a number I knew by heart. After a few rings, a familiar voice crackled through the speaker. "Dr. Margaret Hansen here. How can I assist you today, Charles?"

"Margaret, I need your expertise, something strange has happened in my office. An intruder left behind a doorknob coated with a clear liquid. It could be a poison. I dare not touch it myself. You might be able to shed some light on it. Make sure to bill me for it."

"Poison!" The scientist's interest deepened. "A poison? I must admit, you do have a knack for finding the most intriguing cases." There was a momentary pause on the other end of the line, and then Margaret's voice returned, now laced with curiosity. "I'll be right over, Charles."

True to her word, Dr. Margaret arrived within the hour. She was a brilliant scientist known for her work in chemistry and forensic analysis. Her sharp eyes took in the scene – the doorknob, the office, and my expectant expression.

"Margaret, thanks for coming."

Dr. Margaret Hansen stood there, a striking figure in her mid-thirties, with a mane of chestnut hair that cascaded down to her shoulders. Her piercing blue eyes held a mixture of intelligence and curiosity, and her confident demeanour seemed to draw the room's light towards her.

She wore a tailored, charcoal-gray pantsuit that emphasized her slender frame and exuded an air of professionalism. The crisp white blouse she wore beneath the jacket seemed to contrast perfectly with her richly coloured hair. She carried a leather gladstone bag, undoubtedly carrying an assortment of scientific tools.

I rose from my seat and extended a hand in greeting. Margaret's lips curved into a grin as she accepted my handshake. Her grip was firm, and for the one thousandth time I wondered why I had never made an effort to get to know this lady in a deeper way.

"Jack, you always know how to make a girl feel welcome," she quipped, her voice carrying a hint of playful sarcasm.

I motioned towards my office door. "Well, I've got a puzzle that needs your expertise."

Margaret approached the doorknob, slipping on a pair of latex gloves. She pulled out a small kit from her bag – vials, swabs, and various testing equipment. "Let's find out."

Minutes passed as Margaret meticulously conducted her analysis, while I paced and occasionally peered over her shoulder. Finally, she looked up with a triumphant smile. She tore her gaze away from the vial and turned her attention back to me. "Mind if I set up shop here for a while?"

"Consider my office your play-ground, "I replied with a grin.

For the next hour, the office transformed into a makeshift laboratory. Margaret's scientific instruments meticulously arranged on the desk, I looked on with a mixture of fascination and admiration as she worked, her focus unbroken as she carefully analysed the substance. I had expected her to have to take a sample back to her lab. It had not occurred to me she could do anything in my office.

Carefully, she swabbed a small sample of the clear liquid from the doorknob, sealed it in a vial. After a few minutes of focused work, she glanced up with a thoughtful expression.

"Charles, this substance is some sort of fast-acting paralytic agent, it is designed to be absorbed through the skin upon contact. If my suspicions are correct, a simple touch could cause temporary paralysis."

I was not surprised with that result.

"This is clearly not the work of an amateur."

"Can you determine the origin of this substance?"

Margaret nodded. "I'll run a comprehensive analysis and cross-reference it with any known substances in our database. It might take a bit of time, but I'm confident we'll get some answers."

She got back to me in two hours on the phone. "Charles, I've got something. The composition of this substance matches that of a rare toxin used by some espionage agencies. It is not a substance you would come across every day. It would not have paralysed you; it would have killed you within a few seconds. I will send my assistant over to clean the doorknob. It requires special chemicals."

"I owe you again Margaret."

"No charge, she said, buy me a coffee sometime. I do not get such intriguing investigations in my ordinary work. Be careful Charles."

"Yeah, I said, doing that."

CHAPTER THIRTEEN

I have dealt with my fair share of mysteries and dangers, but what unfolded in my office that day was beyond anything I had encountered before. No doubt about it the heat was on me. I had a choice; backoff or find a way to solve this case quickly. I am not so naïve as to think I can dodge every attempt to silence me. Although with Gods help and my team my chances for survival are way above that of the ordinary private eye.

My team? I have not mentioned them. They are invisible! Before you decide I am certifiable let me explain. The Bible says we are surrounded by an innumerable company of angels. Innumerable means too many to number. Then it says, and I quote: - 'What are the angels, then? They are spirits who serve God and are sent by him to help those who are to receive salvation' -. When I became a Christian I qualified for the help of Angels, I take that seriously. I request their help every-day. The Bible makes clear that uncountable number of angels are more involved in human events than most of us have a clue about.

I do not like to back off. You see, admitting that the weight of those threats is getting to me, that the intimidation is starting to crawl under my skin, it is like giving them the upper hand. No way am I going to let them think they have got me by the throat. So, I play it cool, shrug it off with a smirk and a smart remark. I deflect and dodge, parrying their attempts to rattle me like a seasoned boxer in the ring.

Sure, there are nights when I lie in bed, staring at the ceiling, each creak in the floorboards turning into footsteps of trouble. But I swallow it down, In the past I used whiskey and cigarettes to get me through those nights. Can't do that anymore. The minute I show weakness, the vultures start circling, and this city, they thrive on weakness.

The moment you start acknowledging that the walls are closing in, that the shadows in the alleys feel a bit more suffocating, well, that's the moment you start second-guessing every move, every lead, every person you thought you could trust. I have seen friends go down that road, admitting weakness, showing vulnerability. Next thing you know, they are pushing up daisies. The scum bags think they can just waltz in, these lowlifes, with their cheap threats and intimidation tactics.

Sure, I have stared down the barrel of a gun more times than I care to count. Yeah, I have had whispers of danger brush against my ear like a cold breeze in the dead of night. Am I reluctant to admit I am feeling the pressure? No, it's just how I am wired., presenting an aura of invincibility is what keeps the scum at bay.

So, no, I will not let them see the sweat on my brow or the tremor in my hands. I will wear this mask of indifference, because it's the only way to survive in a world where danger lurks behind every corner. So, I don't back down? It is simple, really.

First off, I am not the type to cower in the face of some two-bit punk trying to play tough. I have had a gun pointed at my head more times than I can remember. But do you know what? I'm still here. I am still breathing, and I'm still standing tall.

Secondly, I have a job to do. People come to me when they are desperate, when they've got nowhere else to turn. They trust me to dig up the truth, to shine a light in the shadows, and to bring justice to a world that often seems devoid of it. If I let every lowlife who throws a threat my way scare me off, I would be letting down the very people who rely on me to make things right.

And let's not forget, I have a reputation to uphold. When word gets around that you are the kind of guy who doesn't flinch, who does not bend under pressure, folks start thinking twice before they mess with you. It's a dangerous game we play, and showing weakness is an invitation for trouble. So, I stand my ground, not just for me, but for the image I have cultivated over the years.

But the most important reason I don't back down is that fear is a chain, my friend. Once you let it wrap around you, it's hard to break free. Every time I face down a threat, every time I look danger in the eye and refuse to blink, I'm reminding myself that I'm still in control. I won't let fear dictate my actions, and I sure won't let some punk with a chip on his shoulder take that away from me.

Of course, none of that prevents me from appearing to back off. Fortunately, the poison grabbed my attention, and I did not destroy the bugs I had discovered. In an ordinary situation I would have trampled them with my heal. To prevent them from receiving a signal, I had them wrapped in tin foil. I unwrapped one of them, and I put it back under my desk where I had found it. They would believe that the device had malfunctioned and restarted. A typical bug occurrence.

I sat at my desk and punched a few numbers on my phone. The bug would pick that up. I followed with a phony conversation to a fictitious person. I spent five minutes telling my fictitious acquaintance about my close call with the poison. I mentioned how it had rattled me and gotten on my nerves. I had decided to drop the case. It was simply not worth it when my life was constantly in danger. The authorities would have to find Amalie. Coming up against thugs with such lethal intent was more than I could handle, and more than I had bargained for. I whined some more, asked the fictitious listener to call me if they could assist me with any work, and then said goodbye.

There was no way of knowing how much that would help, but it was worth a shot. I would leave the bug there for a few days before removing it again. Listeners would think the thing had gone permanently on the blink. I had to remember not to divulge any secrets while it was there. I wrote the word 'BUG' in big letters on a piece of cardboard and sellotaped it to the wall, where I would see it every-time I walked in.

CHAPTER FOURTEEN

What was my next move? I had to find Amalie quickly and get this thing wrapped up. There is another Bible verse I make use of a lot – 'Now if any man of you lacks wisdom, he should ask God, who gives generously to all without finding fault, and it will be given to him.' – Note it is not restricted to Christians. Anyone can ask wisdom of God and he will receive it. I regularly ask for wisdom in my cases. It will not come as a voice from the sky. It will be a good idea, something you had not considered, or the solution to a problem. Often it is only after the fact I realise my prayer had been answered.

I have got myself a small country house that stands alone amidst a sea of green fields. It exudes simplicity and a connection to nature, offering me a serene retreat from the hustle and bustle of city life. Many city people see country living as a lonely existence separated from people contact. I think that shows how much we have lost. Originally, trees, rivers, lakes, fields of grass, flowers, the hum of insects, and country air, are created to replenish the human soul. David confirms that in the book of Psalms when he said, 'He (God) leads me beside the still waters – He makes me to lie down in green pastures – He restores my soul.'

Perched in the heart of the serene countryside, this small house offers an idyllic escape surrounded by nature's finest. On the front porch, I have a couple of weathered rocking chairs. The porch offers a peaceful spot to watch the sunsets. The interior is unpretentious, with plain white walls and well-worn wooden floors. Sunlight filters in through small windows, casting warm patches of light on the floor. A fireplace along one wall providing warmth in the colder months and a touch of nostalgia.

Outside, I dug a small garden, and the block has a mix of wildflowers and shrubs, A narrow gravel path meanders through the property, leading to a small shed at the back. The house is not just a structure; it is a harmonious extension of the landscape, a retreat where the exterior and interior intertwine to provide an experience of serene living. The place captures the essence of its surroundings, inviting you to revel in the beauty of nature's canvas and find solace in its simplicity.

I jolted awake. The bedside clock said 2.50 am. My senses snapping to attention as a muffled sound reached my ears. I lay still for a moment, straining my ears to decipher the source of the noise. My mind shifted into gear, adrenaline coursing through my veins. The room was bathed in shadows. Moonlight seeped through the half-closed blinds, casting long, ghostly fingers across the wooden floor. Someone was in the garage. I had heard the garage roller door being briefly raised.

Years of experience have honed my instincts. I slid out of bed, my bare feet making no sound on the carpeted floor. I moved towards the door. I reached the door to the garage. Gripping the cold metal knob, I turned it with deliberate intent and swung open the door. What met my eyes was an illuminated tableau, like a scene from a noir film brought to life. Moonlight filtered through a small window, casting long shadows that seemed to dance to their own rhythm. And there, at the centre of the makeshift stage, stood a figure, hunched over the heart of my passion – my '67 mustang, a wrench in one hand and a flashlight in the other.

"Freeze!" My voice cut through the silence. The intruder's head snapped up, the flashlight beam momentarily blinding me as it swept over me. This momentary distraction was all the intruder needed. He leapt at me. I saw the glint of the wrench in one hand. I lunged forward, my hand grabbing for the intruder's wrist in a vice-like grip. But he was quick, too, and managed to wriggle free.

"You picked the wrong garage, buddy," I growled. He was a wiry figure clad in dark clothes and a beanie,

My instincts kicked in, and I lunged forward, getting a powerful grip around the intruder's arm. The ensuing struggle was a collision of strength and desperation, each of us fighting for control. Tools clattered to the ground, and the Mustang's pristine paintwork received scratches in the chaos.

The intruder's gaze darted around the garage, assessing his options like a cornered animal. He swung the wrench with surprising force, catching me across the forearm. Pain exploded through the arm, but I managed to hold on, using my shoulder to knock him off balance.

A brief, fierce struggle ensued. My training gave me the upper hand. As a cop I had spent three months in Israel as part of an exchange program. It was an observer roll and allowed me a lot of spare time. I took a course in Krav Maga the Israeli self-defence art. It has no fancy moves or elaborate strategies. Survival in a fight is the main idea with moves aimed at the eyes, throat, groin, and other vulnerable parts of the body. My training kicked in, each action a response to the intruder's unpredictable manoeuvres. I delivered a solid blow to his midsection. a well-placed punch that stole the wind from his lungs. He stumbled back, crashing into the work bench, and knocking over tools in a clatter of chaos.

He broke free from my hold, his elbow connecting with my chest in a painful blow. I stumbled back, my breath hitching, but I was not about to let up. Adrenaline coursed through my veins, a primal force that fuelled my determination.

The thugs' eyes widened, and he bolted towards the garage door. He dropped to the concrete and rolled under the partly opened roller door. I did not want to do that with my painful arm. I raced back into the house and came out the front door.

The intruder had reached my driveway, a dirt track leading down to the sealed road, where a car was parked a short distance away. With adrenaline-fueled speed, I closed the gap between us, but the hoodlum managed to slip into the waiting car. The engine roared to life, and tires screeched as the vehicle peeled away into the night.

I skidded to a stop, my chest heaving as I watched the taillights disappear around a corner. I was left standing in the driveway, a mix of frustration and relief swirling within me. I glanced back at the garage. The rat had been in the process of connecting some explosive device to my car, no doubt intended to detonate when I turned the ignition key. My arm continued to throb, a painful reminder of the struggle.

CHAPTER FIFTEEN

The arm was bruised with no serious injury, in the morning. On the way to work I realised I should have considered two other possibilities in the case a lot earlier than the present. If they were fact, I had been wasting my time. Was Amalie an FBI employee or of the CIA or NSA? She would not be the first journalist to have that identity. Had she been stirring the Medico-Pharma pot at the behest of one of those organizations? Had she been whisked away when things got hot? Was she in a safe house at this moment?

Amalie on the payroll of another Pharmaceutical Company, a competitor of Medi-Pharma, was the second conjecture I had not thought about. That was doubtful. A business competitor would not become involved in clandestine protection of a journalist. My instincts told me the first proposition was also a long shot. The vehement reaction of the partnership of the Company and the thugs towards me was a signal that they had something to hide concerning Amalie Blackwood. I decided to discard those scenarios as possibilities.

I turned into the underground parking area below my building and pulled the Mustang into my usual spot.

A 1967 Mustang in pristine condition is a true embodiment of classic American automotive excellence. Its timeless design and impeccable craftsmanship evoke a sense of nostalgia and admiration among enthusiasts and casual observers alike. From the front, the '67 Mustang presents a confident and commanding stance. The grille is a symmetrical arrangement of horizontal chrome bars, flanked by dual headlights that peer out from recessed housings. The centre of the grille proudly bears the signature Mustang emblem, a galloping horse that signifies the car's spirited nature.

The exterior of my '67 Mustang gleams with a flawless coat of factory-original paint, resplendent in a rich and vibrant hue that captures the essence of the era. The flawless paintwork, until last night, free from imperfections or blemishes, reflects the surrounding environment with a radiant gleam. The chrome accents, from the front grille to the rear bumper, sparkle as if they had just rolled off the assembly line.

The interior is a blend of comfort and vintage charm. The cabin welcomes occupants with plush bucket seats upholstered in premium vinyl, retaining their supple texture and rich colour. The dashboard features an array of analogue gauges, showcasing the simplicity of the time. The wood-grain trim, immaculate steering wheel, and perfectly preserved controls evoke the feeling of stepping back into the 1960s.

Under the hood, a potent V8 engine that roars to life with a deep, rumbling exhaust note. This mechanical marvel, restored to its original specifications, delivers both power and refinement, capable of effortlessly propelling the car down the open road. The engine bay is a showpiece in itself, with every component meticulously detailed and maintained. The curvature of the fenders and the gentle sweep of the rear haunches evoke a sense of motion even while standing still. The pronounced wheel arches house a set of classic-styled, multi-spoke alloy wheels that complement the car's overall aesthetic. The chrome accents, such as the door handles, window trim, and side mirrors, catch the light and add a touch of glamour to the exterior.

Moving to the back of the '67 Mustang, the fastback roofline seamlessly merges into the rear deck, creating a sense of continuity in the design. The taillights are a distinctive triple-segmented arrangement on each side, with chrome surrounds that echo the design language of the front grille. The Mustang lettering is boldly displayed across the rear, leaving no doubt about the car's identity.

Driving the '67 Mustang is an experience that transcends time. The responsive steering, coupled with a finely tuned suspension, provides a connection between driver and machine that modern cars often struggle to replicate. As you press the accelerator, the V8 engine surges with power, launching the car forward with a graceful yet exhilarating motion. The transmission shifts smoothly, capturing the essence of a bygone era of driving. Owning a '67 Mustang in pristine condition is like owning a piece of history – a tribute to the golden age of American muscle cars. Its unblemished exterior, captivating interior, and thrilling performance make it a rolling work of art that commands attention and admiration wherever I go.

In the dimly lit underground carpark, I eased my car into a parking spot and killed the engine. The soft hum of fluorescent lights buzzed overhead, casting eerie shadows that danced around the concrete pillars.

I stepped out of my car and closed the door with a solid thud, the sound echoing through the desolate space. The metallic click of my keys as I locked the vehicle cut through the silence. But a peripheral flicker caught my attention. Between the closely parked cars, obscured but unmistakable, stood a figure. He leaned casually against a dented sedan, exuding a dangerous nonchalance, a towering behemoth of a man. His icy blue eyes produced a menacing glare.

However, this tableau was not as straightforward as the solitary antagonist. Just as I locked eyes with the first figure, another emerged from the shadows to my left. This one leaned against a support pillar, a cigarette dangling from his lips, a second hood of medium height, with neatly slicked back black hair, wearing a finely tailored suit. His attire mirrored that of his counterpart – an unmistakable sign of their affiliation. The situation reeked of a setup, a carefully orchestrated ambush.

These goons were relentless. I guess they had a large pool of punks to draw upon. In frustration I thought, 'come on, do we have to get it on this early in the morning? I have not had my coffee yet.'

Instinct kicked in, my hand sliding toward the reassuring weight of the pistol holstered under my arm. It was a familiar dance; one I had danced before in the grimy back alleys and smoke-filled rooms of this city. I sized up the situation, calculating my odds, ready to make my move.

But fate had other plans that night. Just as I began to piece together my strategy, the world shifted around me. From behind, hands like steel vices clamped onto my arms, immobilizing me. I struggled, but their grip was unrelenting. My gaze followed the curve of a needle, gleaming malevolently in the dim light, before it plunged into my skin.

The effect was immediate. A cold numbness spread from the injection site, tendrils of darkness closing in on the edges of my vision. My limbs grew heavy, the ground tilting beneath me. The battle I had braced for became a distant memory as consciousness slipped through my fingers like sand. The last thing I saw before surrendering to the void was the smile of the big gangster. And then, nothing but darkness.

CHAPTER SIXTEEN

The thumping headache I had when I returned to consciousness was the least of my problems. I was stretched out on an old steel bed without a mattress. The coiled wire springs digging into my back. My arms pulled above my head, had steel shackles on both wrists. Chains went from them to the wall behind me. By twisting my neck, I could just make out the welds where the chains joined the wall. New welds.

I was in my shirt and trousers, and still had my shoes on. Steel shackles encircled my ankles with chains attached to the bed frame. New welds again no doubt. I was in trouble this time. I had accused Amalie Blackwood of being naïve for attempting to take on the business/thug partnership single-handedly. With this outcome, it would be difficult for me to persuade anyone that the same did not apply to myself.

This was the last stop, the end of the line. No smart moves would get me out of this one. I seemed to be inside a freight container. Doors on these things lock from the outside. Not that that made much difference, I would not get to the door anytime soon. The question of air occurred to me. If the container was air-tight, it would be over once I had used all the oxygen available. Ironically, the thought was comforting. Running out of air meant I would slip into unconsciousness and be spared a slow painful death of discomfort and starvation. I had put myself on the wrong side of a nasty bunch of bozos. After an hour and a half of increasing discomfort I slipped into a distraught sleep.

I could have sworn I had been awakened by a hand shaking my shoulder. My searching gaze told me I was still the only resident in the steel box. Then it hit me. My arms were by my side. My legs were free.

Both sets of shackles lay on the floor. I sat up and swung my legs over on to the floor. I sat there dazed for a few minutes. I happened to glance at the door end of my prison. Was I hallucinating all this? One half of that end of the container was slightly ajar. Disappointment would be severe if I were merely dreaming. I put my hand on the bed, it was real enough. I stood, walked over to the far wall, and placed my hand on it. Cold steel.

A familiarity about this experience lingered in my mind. As if it was an event replayed. Then it came to me: The New Testament book of Acts chapter twelve. The apostle Peter lay in prison, chained between two Roman soldiers. An angel woke Peter by striking him on the side, helped him up, the chains fell off, and in effect, said to Peter, "get up, get dressed, and let's go!" Peter thought he was dreaming. I could identify with that! The two of them walked past two guard posts without being seen. The main iron gate of the prison opened of its own accord as Peter and his friend approached it. Stepping out into the street Peter accepted he was not dreaming. He is quoted as saying, "Now I know for certain that the Lord has sent His angel and delivered me,"

I had to say the same. "Now I know the Lord has sent His angel and delivered me." "Thank you," was the only response I could come up with. But it seemed to adequately cover everything. My suit jacket and overcoat lay on the floor. I donned them and made for the exit. I pushed the thing open and barely managed to save myself from plummeting ten meters to the ground. My container, four levels up, was one of hundreds in one of those waterfront container storage depots. Happily, my phone and wallet were still in the inside pocket of my overcoat. The phone display said 1am.

Not much lighting had been wasted on a container holding depot. I had to be extra careful climbing down four levels of stacked containers in the dark. Hand and foot holds were not in abundance. I can testify, coming to what you thought was the end of your existence, tends to make all other problems seem minor. My appreciation for life in general had markedly increased, making an old container graveyard seem like paradise.

I had been handed the advantage. I had ceased to exist in the minds of my enemies. I was not going to push it by returning to my office or home. I began walking. I was not sure what part of town I was in, or if I was in the same town. It did not matter. The nearest Motel would allow me to get some sleep, clean myself up, and make plans. Though I was hungry, stiff, sore, and tired, I could have walked all day on the euphoria of being alive and a free man.

I settled for a truck stop service station with trucker accommodation facilities. It would do for the first twenty-four hours. I purchased two microwave heated burgers, after which I fell into bed, I had a new appreciation for comfortable beds, and slept twelve hours. I had determined I was in a Port locality one hundred kilometres from home.

A thirty-minute hot shower in the morning added to the sense of refreshing a good sleep had given me. A couple of bad dreams told me my mind was still processing the stress of the past twenty-four hours. I did not shave. Altering my appearance with a beard was another safety measure. My clothes were stained and torn in places. Which gave me the idea of changing my usual preferences in clothing. Breakfast was bacon, eggs, and coffee. I paid the bill and got directions to two Motels close by. I hired a cab to view them both and settled on the Rest 4U Inn. I booked in for three days.

CHAPTER SEVENTEEN

I wanted to research the Medico-Pharma Corporation and the CEO. I located a local library with hourly computer hire. I could have done the online search on my phone. I find the screen too small for that purpose. I am more relaxed using a standard desktop monitor. On route to the library, I did some shopping. I emerged from thirty minutes in a menswear store wearing a tweed jacket with leather elbow patches, charcoal woollen trousers, dark brown dress shirt, crimson woollen tie, and tan brogue shoes. With a full growth of beard, I would look more like a history professor than a P.I. I may make the change permanent. Definite benefits go along with a P.I. not looking like a P.I. My soiled clothes and shoes went into a public rubbish bin.

A back copy of Business Dynamics Monthly Magazine had a feature on Medico-Pharma and the CEO Henry Kincaid. Medico-Pharma described as a beacon of business excellence and Mr. Kincaid as the enigmatic and charismatic CEO. 'Under Henry Kincaid's visionary leadership, the company's commitment to research and development is evident in their portfolio of life-changing drugs that have garnered global recognition. Kincaid's innate ability to balance business acumen with a passion for societal well-being has turned Medico-Pharma into a powerhouse in the pharmaceutical sector.'

'Beyond the boardroom, Kincaid's penchant for luxury takes centre stage, most notably with his extravagant seafaring escapades. The CEO is often spotted cruising the cerulean waters surrounding the Greek islands aboard his majestic super yacht, appropriately christened "Elysium." This floating emblem of opulence is a testament to Kincaid's unabashed embrace of the finer things in life.'

'Kincaid's yacht serves as a passport to explore the Greek islands in unparalleled style. While most CEOs opt for exclusive resorts, Kincaid's love affair with the islands extends to mingling with the locals, savouring authentic cuisine, and experiencing the culture firsthand. It's this down-to-earth charm coupled with extravagant living that adds another layer to Kincaid's mystique.'

To keep up such a business and personal front, Kincaid would be utilising corrupt powerful connections in high places. My next step was a few days of surveillance of the Elysium. I figure, where there is a yacht, there is bound to be some action. Parties, gatherings, you name it. I cancelled the further two days at the Inn, hired a car, and drove the hundred kilometres back to the city. Again, taking extra safety measures, I would be hiring a different car every few days. The expenses in the case were escalating. Eventually I would fill Sam Blackwood in on my adventures, and we could thrash out a fair sum.

I took up a position on a hill overlooking the Marina yacht moorings. Down below, the tranquil harbor stretched out like a sapphire jewel nestled within the embrace of the coastline. The gentle waves danced in harmonious rhythm, their crests shimmering with the radiant touch of the sun's golden fingers. The air carried the faint tang of salt, mingling with the sweet fragrance of blooming flowers that adorned the hillsides.

My position was above and far enough away from the Marina that it was doubtful I would be noticed. On the other hand, who knows what security measures were on the yacht. What surveillance they maintained. With all the hanky-panky Kincaid and his partners were up to it made sense they would have lookouts posted. I would be using binoculars. I purchased an easel, a canvas, and a set of paints and brushes as a cover for my activity. I hope you have a fat wallet, Sam! I would have to fiddle around and make it look as if I was using the binoculars for close ups, then recording it on my canvas. Not having access to my clothing at home meant further purchase of casual wear suited to a hobby painter.

At the heart of this nautical tableau lay an assembly of yacht moorings, a mesmerizing collection of sleek vessels tethered to the world of leisure and extravagance. The yachts varied in size and design, each one a reflection of its owner's distinct taste and affluence. Sunlight bathed the polished hulls, turning them into dazzling beacons that beckoned to the onlooker's senses.

Yet, amongst this symphony of maritime elegance, one yacht stood apart, the Elysium, a true masterpiece of maritime engineering and luxury. It was as if a sculptor's hand had expertly chiselled its form from the sea itself. A gleaming hull, painted in a shade of deep midnight blue, seemed to absorb and mirror the azure sky above, creating a seamless blend of sea and air.

The yacht's lines were a symphony of grace and power, a testament to the seamless fusion of artistry and technology. A trio of majestic decks soared upward, providing a canvas for relaxation and indulgence. The uppermost deck, crowned by a billowing sun canopy, hosted an array of plush seating and lounge chairs, inviting passengers to recline in lavish comfort while soaking up the panorama.

A cascade of floor-to-ceiling windows adorned the mid-deck, revealing glimpses of an interior that could only be described as opulent splendour. I could make out crystal chandeliers, and lavish furnishings in silk and velvet. Every inch of space meticulously designed to envelop its occupants in a cocoon of elegance and refinement.

The lowermost deck, seemingly dipping its toes into the lapping waves, revealed a state-of-the-art marina. Jet skis and water toys were neatly arranged, ready to be unleashed upon the glittering sea. A hydraulic platform awaited its cue, promising to convey jetsetters into a world of aquatic adventure.

As the sun's rays lingered upon this resplendent vessel, it became an embodiment of dreams realized, a floating sanctuary for the discerning few. It stood as a beacon of aspiration, a testament to the heights of human ingenuity and desire for the extraordinary. And from the vantage point of the hill, I could not help but feel a twinge of envy for those fortunate enough to call such a masterpiece their own. She was a beauty all right. The problem was, dirty money had purchased it. This was the floating palace of Henry Kincaid.

About 2pm my pulse quickened when I spotted the big man himself strolling up the gangway, flanked by his two meathead henchmen. Antonio 'Razor' Moretti, notorious in these parts, his reputation slicing through the criminal underworld like... well, a razor. No wonder I had hit a brick wall of trouble. Moretti was as mean as they come, the worst type of lowlife.

A slow exhale hissed through my clenched teeth as I focused the binoculars on the trio. Razor was decked out in his trademark pinstriped suit, a sinister grin etched on his mug like a permanent scar. His goons, followed close, like obedient bloodhounds ready to sink their teeth into whatever scraps Razor tossed their way.

They disappeared into the yacht's belly, like rats scuttling into a hole. I was witnessing a meeting of predators. Day gave way to evening. As the moon cast its silvery gaze upon this floating masterpiece, it became a vessel of fantasies realized, an embodiment of luxury that embraced the night with open arms. It stood as a testament to the allure of the unknown, a promise of escapades waiting to unfold beneath the star-studded canvas. And from the vantage point of the hill, I could not help again but feel a sense of wonderment, as if I were witnessing a secret world illuminated only for those with the eyes to see.

As night set in the shimmering lights of the harbor danced upon the water's surface, creating a mesmerizing ballet of reflections that wove a tapestry of starlit dreams. The distant glow of coastal towns painted a constellation of their own, each light a distant ember that beckoned with the promise of stories untold. The scent of brine hung in the air, mingling with the gentle caress of a night breeze that carried with it the hint of adventure.

The yacht moorings twinkled like a treasure trove of jewels, the reflections of their lights shimmered upon the water like liquid stardust, weaving a celestial path towards the open sea.

The Elysium's decks were an interplay of gentle radiance and shadow, a dance of contrasts that whispered of hidden wonders within. The uppermost deck, adorned with delicate fairy lights, created a celestial pathway leading to plush seating where passengers could recline beneath the canopy of stars.

Amid the nocturnal symphony of the mid-deck, the interior's windows were like portals into a world of enchantment. The warm glow of cabin lights revealed glimpses of the lavish furnishings their hues a palette of midnight blues and velvety purples. The chandeliers dangled like constellations brought to life, casting a soft luminescence upon rich wooden accents and intricate artwork.

The lowest deck, now an aquatic tableau of softly lit elegance. The water toys, now silhouetted by the shimmering sea, awaited their turn to dance upon the waves. The hydraulic platform, now a stage of shimmering liquid. Soft tunes began to drift out. They were preparing for an onboard party. Taxis and limousines began to arrive creating a steady stream of guests moving up the gang plank. A helicopter touched down briefly on the Helipad at the rear of the vessel, disgorged its passengers, and lifted off again.

For an hour or so I attempted to identify some of the rich and possibly famous, but it was difficult to do with a crowd on board and the interplay of shadows and light all over the boat. My patience was wearing thin. I had been on the hill since 9am and it was midnight. I had confirmed an alliance between Kincaid and the lead gangster in this part of the country. It did not though, get me any closer to finding Amalie Blackwood. I made the decision to pack up my easel and blank canvas and return to my Motel. Then I spotted an answer to prayer. I recognized one of the dancers on the upper deck.

CHAPTER EIGHTEEN

It was twenty minutes before I was certain. Eva Bulgari was an NSA operative. She had to be on an undercover assignment. It was comforting to know the NSA at least was keeping tabs on these boys. Depending on how deep her cover was, if I could touch base with Eva, I might get a lead regarding Amalie. Tired and irritable though I was, I had to stay at my perch on the hill until I saw Eva leave the boat. That meant constant vigilance with the binoculars trained on the gangplank. I carried the art gear down to the car and returned to keep my eyes peeled.

In any sane employment, I would be on triple time with bonuses by now. I had to keep reminding myself I was doing this in the hope of saving a woman's life. Keeping my eyes open was proving to be a problem. More than once I nodded off. My reward came at 3.30 am, Eva came down the gangplank alone and entered one of the cabs lined up on the dock. I raced for the car. The cab sped past as I arrived at the intersection with the access road. I dipped my headlights and followed, keeping well back. Forty-five minutes later when the cab turned into a suburban driveway, I drove past, pulled to the side of the road further on, opened my door, jumped the low fence, and ran into the stand of trees edging the property. Eva was on the veranda searching her bag for her keys when I drew level with the house.

I stayed in the shadow of the trees and called "Eva!"

As I had expected her hand went straight into the bag, reaching for her gun.

"Eva, its Charles Winston, remember me?"

She relaxed a little. I figured she could not see me clearly. The hand stayed in the bag. "Yes Charles, how could I forget that week we spent on the Henderson case in Chicago."

"Yeah Eva, I said, except it was two days, not a week. It was the Halliburton case, and it was in New York."

"How are you, Charles? What do you want.?"

"I don't want to compromise you in any way Eva. I'll stay in the shadows. I'm in P.I. work now. I need a lead, just one lead regarding the disappearance of Amalie Blackwood."

"I can't promise anything Charles. Give me three days. If I come up with anything I will leave a single slip of paper folded, under the foot of the statue of the unknown soldier in the city. No paper means I was not successful."

"Thanks Eva, I owe you one."

I went back to my car and drove to the Motel.

CHAPTER NINETEEN

Over the following two days I emailed Sam Blackwood saying I was having considerable opposition but was still on the case. He would hear from me as soon as I had something certain. I contacted the security company responsible for my office building, said I was unavoidably detained, would not be in the office for some-time, asked them to wheel clamp the Mustang, keep a close eye on it, and bill me for the service.

On the third day I drove to the city early and ate breakfast on the balcony of the hotel opposite the statue of the unknown soldier. Ordering coffee hourly to keep the management happy, I watched for Eva's arrival. At 11 a.m., she approached the statue, made a pretence of admiring it, and surreptitiously tucked the paper under the foot. Great! Maybe a positive lead at last towards finding Amalie Blackwood.

I finished my third cup of coffee and stood to leave, I stopped short when I noticed a guy in a dark suit and sunglasses walk to the statue, retrieve the slip of paper, read it, pocket it, and walk away. Eva had a tail. Almost certainly that indicated they were wise to her clandestine activity. The least I could do was warn her.

Returning to her house was the only way I had to contact her. I drove to the house at midnight, parked well down the street, jumped the fence again, and approached through the trees. I slipped up to the veranda quickly, and pushed a note, in an envelope marked with the letter E, under the front door. If Eva was not the only resident it might cause problems for her. I could do nothing else. The note said, 'Eva – Charles - you have a tail. I was watching from across the street. A bozo in a suit and sunglasses retrieved the paper before I got to it. I am at room 12 – Sunset Motel.'

A knock at the Motel room door woke me at 6 am. I opened to find Eva with a suitcase. I welcomed her in. "Thanks Charles, you probably saved my life."

"Glad to be of service. Do you think the NSA will compensate me – pen, note paper, petrol, and two hours night work?"

She smiled. "I doubt it."

I grinned. "Me too."

"Charles, I'm not going back there. Can I sleep on the couch until I send in a report, and get new instructions?"

"Sure, no problem. Oh, by the way, what was on the paper?"

"The Greek Island Santorini."

"Really! Also called Thira?"

Eva nodded. "The word is they are holding her somewhere on the Island."

Later I had dressed and was contemplating breakfast. Eva looked me up and down. "What's with the beard Charles, and the clothes. That's not your preferred choice of clothing is it.?"

I shook my head. "No, Moretti's crew have been giving me a lot of grief. I have the advantage now. They think I'm dead. I am taking no chances though, hence the beard and change of dress. I'm staying away from home and the office for the time being. I'll tell you about it sometime."

"Eva, I assume you did some intricate NSA moves to ensure you were not followed here?"

Eva Laughed. "I did not have too. One of them was in a car not far from the house, but he was asleep, so I made a clean getaway."

"Charles, you will be travelling to Santorini.?"

"Yes, I hope to. It's my first solid lead since I started on the case. I'll need the approval of my client. His expenses will go sky high. On the other hand, we are talking about the life of his sister."

"What do you think about a partnership, she said, You and I? The publicity if we find her will go a long way to exposing Medico-Pharma and their hoodlum allies. I am sure my superiors will agree if I put it to them that way. We have contacts in the Greek Police (ELAS) and the Greek Secret Service (EYP)"

"Sounds good Eva." Secretly I was dancing for joy. It was more than I could hope for. The NSA and the Greek authorities backing my lone investigation.

I sent Sam Blackwood a text. 'Sam, Amalie is imprisoned on the Greek Island Thira. I am happy to travel there. I will have the assistance of the NSA, and through them the Greek Police and the Greek Security Services. Your expenses will rise rapidly?'

Sam came back to me with two words; 'Do it.' Thirty minutes later he sent a message asking for my bank details and offering to deposit two thousand dollars as a part payment. I sent the details and expressed my appreciation.

CHAPTER TWENTY

Eva checked with her superiors and received the green light. Eva is a small athletic woman who exudes an air of intensity and purpose. Standing at around 5'5" (165 cm), her compact frame belies her capabilities. My work with Eva in the past had revealed her as a force to be reckoned with. Her short, raven-black hair pulled back in a practical yet stylish manner. Her eyes are a striking shade of deep green. She favours form-fitting clothing that does not hinder her movement. An accomplished Martial arts practitioner, weapons, and survival equipment expert, she carries herself with the poise of someone who has been through countless high-pressure situations and emerged victorious. A more competent partner I could not hope to find in the dangerous activity ahead of us.

NSA assistance proved to be invaluable. Eva had knocked on my door Tuesday morning. Thursday evening the two of us were aboard a Military flight to Athens. Meals, beverages, and first-class comfort were missing. I had no complaints. The flight was Gratis. Although I carried my Passport; Visa's, Passports, and other travel documents had been waved. We were entering Greece as Military personnel. A ten-hour flight saw us over Athens early morning. As the aircraft gradually descended the vast expanse of the Aegean Sea came into view, stretched out on one side.

The Military Transport approached Athens from the east, affording us a breathtaking panoramic view. The Acropolis, crowned by the majestic Parthenon, rose like a guardian above the urban sprawl. The bustling Plaka neighbourhood, with its narrow alleys and vibrant colours, painted a vivid picture of Athens' vibrant culture. The modern city centre, a juxtaposition of contemporary architecture and historical landmarks, highlighted the evolution of a city deeply rooted in its heritage. With the city now fully in view, the aircraft began its descent towards the military airfield with the thrumming of the aircraft's landing gear.

Two representatives, one of ELAS, the other of the EYP, waited as we disembarked. On the flight Eva and I had agreed initially we would split up. Eva would do her NSA thing in Athens, whatever that was, for a few days, and I would go directly to Santorini posing as a wandering tourist. The possibility of Eva being recognized because of the length of time she had been undercover was there. Also, they knew what she had written on the paper from the statue, and because of that might be expecting her to turn up on the island. I on the other hand would be incognito because of the event in the container. The beard and different apparel added to that, made it highly unlikely any of the bad guys, if they were on the island, would pick up on my true identity.

Eva would ring me when she arrived on the island. My objective on the island was to ferret out Amalie's place of captivity. I was counting on the fact of a small community such as was on Santorini, and the human penchant for gossip, to provide me with the answer. I could have flown to the island; it was a two-hour flight. Instead, I chose the eight-hour ferry cruise. It would help me to acclimatized to this new country and the people. The ferry ride typically departs from the port of Piraeus, the main port of Athens, and the duration of the trip can vary depending on the type of ferry you choose. Both high-speed ferries and slower traditional ferries are available, each offering a different balance between speed and comfort. The traditional ferries provided the experience I was seeking.

As the ferry departs from Piraeus, passengers are treated to views of the bustling port area, with ships of various sizes and shapes lining the docks. As the ferry moves away from the mainland, the blue expanse of the Aegean Sea stretches out in all directions. During the journey I had a choice of onboard amenities such as cafes, restaurants, and seating areas, where one can relax and take in the view. Many ferries also have outdoor decks that allow passengers to feel the refreshing sea breeze and capture some incredible photos of the surrounding waters.

Overall, the ferry trip from Athens to Santorini is not just a means of transportation; it is an integral part of the journey that allows travellers to appreciate the beauty of the Aegean Sea, the Cyclades islands, and the stunning landscape of Santorini itself. Santorini is renowned for its breathtaking sunsets, white-washed buildings, and unique geological features.

As the ferry approaches Santorini, the island's iconic white buildings and blue domes become visible against the dramatic backdrop of the caldera—a submerged volcanic crater. The sight is truly awe-inspiring, and the contrast between the deep blue sea and the brilliant white architecture creates a postcard-perfect scene.

The ferry docks at Athinios Port, which is located at the base of the steep cliffs that characterize Santorini's coastline. From there, passengers disembark and have the option to take a bus or taxi to their final destination within the island, whether it's the capital town of Fira, the charming village of Oia, or any of the other picturesque settlements. As a first-time visitor I had no idea where to start. I asked the driver of a blue vintage Mercedes Benz taxi, a fellow with a warm smile, deep tan, and ragged beard, who greeted me with "Kalispera!" to take me to Fira. I said I wanted accommodation not to cheap, and not too expensive, which I demonstrated with that rocking back and forth of the hand every European knows the meaning of.

CHAPTER TWENTY ONE

I was hoping such mid-level lodgings would keep me in touch with the common people. Fira was perched on the edge of a steep volcanic cliff overlooking the azure waters of the Aegean. Its principal features are flat roofed whitewashed buildings, blue domed churches, and narrow winding streets. Fira's streets wind their way through the town in a maze of narrow alleys and paths. The paths often lined with shops, restaurants, and cafes.

The driver whose name was Nikos, left me at a guesthouse near the town centre. My room had comfortable furnishings with a touch of Greek décor, and included modern amenities, air conditioning, private bathroom, and a balcony to soak in the views. Topped off with warm and friendly service. Nikos had offered me his services as an interpreter. I took his contact number. How much English was spoken on the island I did not know. I figured two days would make it clear if I needed Nikos' help.

I rung Nikos the next day. It had occurred me, his position as a cab driver put him in a unique position to have an intimate knowledge of the island and the community. Hopefully that knowledge might save me days of wandering the island asking veiled questions. That afternoon Nikos and I sat in a quaint café sipping on strong Greek coffee. I had offered to hire him as an interpreter, and source of general information about the island.

I decided to plunge in and ask Nikos what he knew about Medico-Pharma. His eyes widened with surprise. He gave me a penetrating stare. "Maybe you are more than an ordinary tourist, eh?" I shrugged and smiled. I waited.

Nikos glanced around before lowering his voice. "They and their friends are dangerous people. They have their claws deep in this island. People have gone missing before, you know."

"Who are their friends?"

"Criminals."

"If they had a prisoner, where would they hold him?"

Nikos sat back in his chair scratching his beard. "There's an old building in the north of the island. Some say strange things happen there."

"Can we go there in the taxi?"

Silence for a moment. Then. "Ok, but we do not stop. We drive past."

I nodded.

Why Medico-Pharma had a presence on Santorini was a mystery to me. Perhaps it had something to do with smuggling. The Greek Islands have been a historically strategic location for smuggling due to their proximity to both Europe and Asia, as well as their numerous islands and extensive coastline. Greece is a country with a vast coastline and numerous islands in the Aegean and Ionian Seas. This geographical layout makes it challenging for authorities to monitor and control all entry points, providing opportunities for smugglers to operate discreetly. Smuggling routes in the Greek Islands are diverse. Some involve land borders with neighbouring countries, such as Turkey and Albania. Others involve sea routes, with smugglers using small boats and vessels to transport people or goods across the Aegean Sea. The proximity of the Greek Islands to Turkey is another factor, with smugglers exploiting the porous maritime border between the two countries.

Nikos was to pick me up at 9am the next morning. On Greek island time I could expect him to turn up anytime between 9am and 11am. A forty-kilometre drive took the rest of the day. Nikos insisted we stop at tourist spots on the way. At some we exited the cab and strolled around for ten minutes. "I make it look like I am showing you the island, it is safer, yes!"

Near Baxedes, at the far north of the island, we came to the isolated old building Nikos called Villa Eolos. Sitting atop a high point overlooking a small cove, its timeworn stones forming a fortress-like structure. The building had traces of Venetian architecture that hinted at its bygone grandeur. Over the years, wind and weather had turned the exterior to a muted Gray. A wire mesh fence encircled it.

"Smugglers, they use this place," Nikos interjected, as the old taxi bumped past on the unsealed road.

"Nikos, do you know anybody who works at Villa Eolos?" "I want to know if they have a prisoner, and the name on any boxes stored there."

Nikos threw up a hand. "Me rótise káti dýskolo!" Remembering I had no idea what he had said, he repeated, "You ask a hard thing!"

Nikos remained silent for ten minutes as we drove back to Fira. Finally, he broke the silence with, "I will try to get the information. I must be careful, it is dangerous."

I paid Nikos the amount we had agreed upon on our arrival at the guest house, including the previous day. I added a substantial tip in appreciation of Nikos' willingness to help.

He came to the guest house at lunchtime the next day. As we sat eating the popular Greek lunchtime meal, Moussaka, he glanced around, then in a low voice, "my friend says yes, they have a prisoner, a woman. Many boxes are there with the name Medico-Pharma."

Bingo! The jackpot! Nikos left, gratified I had made his wallet a little fatter. But not before he had stipulated, "No more information Charles. You have increased my wealth, but a dead man cannot spend money!"

CHAPTER TWENTY TWO

I sent a message to Eva at the email address she had given me. I said I had confirmed a female prisoner being held at Villa Eolos, gave its approximate location, that it was a depot for smugglers, and had in storage boxes bearing the Medico-Pharma brand.

At 7 o'clock, an email from Eva arrived. Tomorrow at precisely 7 am a contingent of Greek Police would arrive by helicopter at Villa Eolos. Eva would accompany them. At 5.30 am, a Mr. Dimitriou from the Santorini Island Police was to pick me up from the guest house. He would use GPS technology to guide the chopper to the precise location upon our arrival at Villa Eolos.

The operation had been meticulously planned. Early morning judged the best time for the element of surprize. The helicopter, painted matte black, came in low, the pilot executed a precision hover, and the officers silently rappelled down to the rooftop of the building. The team dressed in specialized gear designed for both stealth and protection. Doors were broken down and locks picked. The occupants caught off guard by the early morning assault, put up little resistance. Shots reverberated briefly through the compound. Utilizing their training and teamwork the invading force soon gained the upper hand.

As the first light of dawn began to break over the Aegean Sea, the officers emerged from the compound with prisoners in tow. A medical chopper touched down and I had my first view of Amalie Blackwood. She appeared fragile, her hair hung in tangled, matted strands, falling unkempt around her shoulders. Her clothes torn and soiled. Dirt and grime marred her face, her eyes dull and hollow, dark circles underscored them, haunted by the trauma she had endured. I watched as she was assisted to lie on one of the stretchers. The medical helicopter lifted off headed for Athens and Hospital.

CHAPTER TWENTY THREE

I pulled out my Phone and sent a text to Sam Blackwood. 'Amalie safe and in the hands of the Athens Police. You will have to contact them for further information.' Eva and I caught the ferry back to Athens. Two days later we were on another Military flight home. The next item on Eva's to do list was a press release to bring the media running to hear the full story on Amalie Blackwood's kidnapping, Medico-Pharma's involvement, criminal connections, and illicit activities. No amount of political manipulation, legal intimidation, charitable façade, or high-powered lobbying would stop the tsunami about to engulf Henry Kincaid and his cronies. Corrupt players in the regulatory bodies, political circles, and anywhere else would soon be running for cover.

I requested Eva leave me out of the story entirely. On Santorini Nikos knew my name but I had not told him I was a private investigator, and I had used my own name at the guest house. Nowhere near enough to alert the Medico-Pharma Moretti partnership to the fact I was alive. The beard would stay and the change of clothing preference. A quiet return to my home and office and the resumption of business was the plan. The goons would not be keeping an eye out for signs of a dead man. Sam Blackwood had added a considerable sum to his first deposit in my bank account making my first case a financial success.

I had a new appreciation of a small verse in the Bible. It is in the Psalms; 'blessed is the man who has the God of Jacob for his helper.' Relying on that help, I am moving into the future, taking it one day at a time.

ROSS THOMPSON

www.ingramcontent.com/pod-product-compliance
Lightning Source LLC
Chambersburg PA
CBHW051259160726
47994CB00003B/1237